Ivan Gabriel, a 25-year-old literary enthusiast born in Serbia, is a promising author whose passion for literature has been a guiding force throughout his life. Having successfully completed his studies in English literature and linguistics, Ivan's academic background laid the foundation for his deep understanding of language and storytelling. His lifelong love for literature inspired him to embark on a creative journey, culminating in the publication of his debut work. With a unique voice and a fresh perspective, Ivan Gabriel is poised to make a significant impact in the literary world.

To S, for always letting me know that pushing for your dreams is never a blind pursuit, no matter how crazy they may be.

Ivan Gabriel

THE SYSTEM

AUSTIN MACAULEY PUBLISHERS™

LONDON • CAMBRIDGE • NEW YORK • SHARJAH

A CIP catalogue record for this title is available from the British Library.

ISBN 9781035836857 (Paperback)
ISBN 9781035836864 (ePub e-book)

www.austinmacauley.com

First Published 2024
Austin Macauley Publishers Ltd®
1 Canada Square
Canary Wharf
London
E14 5AA

Part one

The protagonist woke up on a day seemingly like all the rest. He went to the toilet, drank his tea, and made the same breakfast as he always does: two pieces of toast with three scrambled eggs. He was not a particularly happy man, but he could have been called content. With a stable job and a set future, he rarely had any real worries other than some menial and boring tasks which must be completed. For example, on this day he had a letter he had to send. He spent his breakfast looking at the letter at hand, not really pondering much. While stuffing the last piece of egg in his mouth, he realised that this was the first time that he would be sending a letter. Indeed, he had never done the task before. *Very interesting*, he thought as he put on his coat. He believed that surely there is a system in place, as there is for everything, which will make this task straightforward.

Walking down the street with a pleased look on his face, he waved and greeted many passers-by, who returned the wave. Upon greeting one man, he did not get a greeting back in return, but the man continued starring at him with a psychotic glance as if he were studying the features of his face very closely. He also noticed that the man was not walking in a straight line, as everybody else was; instead, he was veering from side to side very unsteadily. As he turned from him, he could still feel the heat of his gaze on the back of his head. He felt very uneasy at this occurrence, but gave it no mind as he saw the post office and was edging closer to it. Upon entering, after genially greeting the guard, he saw that there was a line in place. He stood at the back of it with a feeling of relief. *Isn't it lovely that we have systems such as these to help us navigate such a complex society which we have created?* he thought. He watched the people in the line, all of them seemingly moving closer to their goal, each of them following the state of things, following the unsaid laws of the systems that keep society intact. As he edged closer to his desired outcome, he felt a sense of accomplishment, a sense of himself belonging to something bigger, a sense of meaning.

Finally, in no time at all, as the line was moving at a steady and healthy pace, he came face to face with the clerk. He proudly gave the letter to her, which she offhandedly received, and started typing right away. Upon looking at the letter for the first time she gave him an indignant glance.

"There is no name or address on the letter," she said.

"Oh, I am terribly sorry," said the protagonist while slightly blushing. "To be completely frank, this is actually my first time sending a letter, so I am not aware of the protocol."

"Well, this is now a problem. You will have to fill out some papers which explain why you made this mistake and which will show you the way in which it can be corrected."

"Excuse me?" said the protagonist, honestly confused, "Couldn't you just give me the letter now so that I can write the name and address down?"

"No,"

The protagonist felt a cold sweat; he looked back and saw that a line of considerable length had formed, all because of his tribulations. He felt ashamed but still resolved to get to the bottom of this perplexing situation. He wondered if this was just a bad day for the clerk, so he decided to ask again.

"But it would be much easier for both of us and even quicker if I just write it right away. I don't believe there is a need for any paperwork to be involved," he said with a placating smile.

"Sir, I did not make up the rules, but I do know them, and I don't intend to break them. And those rules clearly state that you are to fill out all the necessary forms before you are allowed to send the letter," said the clerk, this time with an air of authority.

The protagonist was not happy with this turn of events, but glancing back he saw that an astoundingly big line had formed behind him, so he reluctantly took the required forms and stepped aside to a table in order to fill them out. Upon first look, the forms seemed very straightforward and easy to fill out. They needed his name, the name of the receiver, their addresses, etc. However, while turning the many pages of the forms he realised that all of them were the same. Each page required the same information, leaving him with the tedious task of filling it all out again and again. Nevertheless, he filled it all out meticulously and went back in line. This time the line seemed to move much slower, and he started feeling anxious. "I could have been done half an hour ago if they had a better system." Out of sheer boredom, he started noticing the other people in line; they seemed to don a strange, satisfied, yet perplexed look on their faces, which he couldn't quite discern.

His musings were interrupted by him being the next one in line.

"Here, all done," the protagonist proudly exclaimed.

The clerk wordlessly took the forms and, without looking at them, placed them in the trash can. The protagonist was horrified, barely containing his rage he kept staring at the clerk until finally, he caught her glance.

"Could you tell me what was the point of me filling out all of those forms for you to just throw them in the trash?" he said, trying to keep his cool.

"That's the protocol."

"I see. And what is the point of me filling out the same form over and over again? Why not just one?"

"That's the system we have, if you would like to make a complaint, you will have to come on a Sunday between 2 and 3 to speak to the manager. But to do that, there are some forms which need to be filled."

The protagonist forced a smile, asked if his letter was sent, and upon receiving confirmation, he left the post office. He felt very upset; he felt betrayed. In the morning, he sang the laurels of the systems of society, only for them to bite him back in such a cruel way. *Was I wrong? Is it not as organised as I might have thought?* These thoughts sprang into his mind ceaselessly. He could not stop thinking about better ways to handle such incidents in the post office. It seemed preposterous to him, forcing people to go through such tedious tasks. He felt crowded by these thoughts and short of breath; his vision became blurry, and suddenly something snapped. It's as if he could hear the snap, but it relieved him of his aches. He felt as if waking up from a long dream. His mind became clear; everything seemed apparent and inexplicable at the same time. The feeling was ineffable. It gave him a very sturdy resolve, but he could not tell for which purpose that resolve was given. Seeing clearly now, he saw that he had wandered too far in the wrong direction and that he would be late for work. He quickly course-corrected and sped up his step in the right direction. While walking, people started greeting him, regular people just passing by, yet they seemed incredibly strange. A permanent grin seemed to be imprinted on their face, a grin that seemed supernatural and eerie. They seemed very content, each of them content and clueless. *What are they so happy about? How can they not see that they are not so? It's a mirage.* These words seemed to stab like a knife into the mind of the protagonist; they stuck in with an air of permanence. "A mirage." He sped up his step, anxious to arrive at work at once. He felt like a revelation had fallen into his lap, a divine countenance, and wished to share it with somebody. *But who? Yes, I know.* He had always thought of his boss as the most level-headed person he knew. Her ability to see every problem clearly and more importantly, solve it was second to none. *Yes, she is the one. I must try and communicate this ineffable revelation to her.*

Upon entering the office, he saw his boss looking at him.

"You're late," she said.

"I know, I apologise," said the protagonist, "but, I have a very good reason, and also, I would like to talk to you about something."

"I don't care about your reason; you are late, and the rules say that you should not be late," said the boss listlessly.

"As I said I am sorry about that," the protagonist was starting to get nervous.

His boss looked at him for a couple of seconds, then turned around and started marching to her desk.

"Wait!" screamed the protagonist, "I wanted to talk to you about something."

"Okay."

"Well, you see today I went to the post office to send a letter," the protagonist was very uneasy; his boss was staring at him with a fish-like expression, devoid of any emotion or understanding. "They made me jump through all these ridiculous hoops just to send a letter."

"Did you make a mistake?"

The protagonist felt chills going down his back; he thought he might have misjudged this woman and that she was in cahoots with the people from the post office.

"Well, yes, but that is not the point," he felt a surge of newfound resolve, "don't you think that these systems are a little bit arbitrary? Don't you think that we all seem to follow these rules just because we don't give them another thought? I mean take for example this situation today: I arrived late at work, but why does there have to be a specific time for work? Why can't we all just work when each of us wants to, as long as the work gets finished, who cares? I mean, wouldn't that just be a lor easier, for everyone? But that's not the point I'm trying to make exactly. There are a lot of things which could be done more effectively. For example, imagine if everybody who wanted to send a letter at the post office could call and have an exact time scheduled for them in order to perform their task. That would be so much easier, don't you think?"

While talking, he was looking into the empty space just in front of his boss, but when he finished his final sentence and the focus shifted back to her face; he felt chills once more.

She was staring at him with an inhuman face, much like the people on the street, but this time without a grin. It was as if an invisible set of hands was holding her face in place while she was helpless to control the movements of it.

"You arrived late," she pronounced coldly, every word accented with an air of finality.

He realised that he was beaten. There was no arguing or chances of an appeal to reason. And to think that he thought that she would be the one to hear out his concerns and revelations and might even have an answer to them. Defeated, he turned around on the way to his desk.

"Wait," he heard behind him. "There are some forms you have to fill out, explaining why you are late to work."

He snapped.

"What? What kind of forms? Why would I do that?"

"It's the protocol."

"Is anybody ever going to read those forms, or use them in any way?"

"No."

"Then what's the point of them?" said the protagonist, grinding his teeth out of rage; he wanted to jump and grab his boss by her shoulders, shake her until she would provide an answer to his question. She did give him an answer, but it was not the one he wanted.

"It's the protocol."

At this point, she stopped giving him the time of day. She turned around, grabbed the forms, and handed them to him. Defeated and disheartened, the protagonist made his way to his desk. He couldn't remember ever feeling quite this way. He felt depressed but yet furious at the same time. Furious because nobody actually looked like they wanted to hear him out, depressed because he felt like they couldn't even if they wanted to. *How can they not see? It's as if someone is controlling their lives for them, unbeknownst to them,* the protagonist mused. Once again, he could not stop this train of thought entering his mind. He felt as if a dam had broken and by breaking let out all the pent-up water behind it, like these thoughts were always there in the background but being held down and pushed back. He started looking at his colleagues around the office. They all displayed that seemingly fake grin on their faces that he started noticing earlier. All of them so set on their tasks, but not thinking about anything for more than five seconds before doing it, not pondering the true nature of things, and more importantly, their purpose. They were like monkeys to him, typing away, writing, mating, being content, without noticing the metal bars around them, prancing around, as animals in a zoo. Images and sounds started crowding his head; he could hear his blood pumping, his heart beating, a cacophony of noises, and other stimuli overwhelming him. He thought he could hear a voice clearing through the noise.

"Did you finish the paperwork for the deadline today?"

"What?" answered the protagonist wearily. He looked up; one of his coworkers was standing next to his desk.

"Did you finish it? I need it so that I can finish my paperwork," he said.

"I'll do it after the lunch break."

"Thanks."

"Wait," the protagonist hesitated a little. "Do you ever think about the purpose of our job?"

"What do you mean? The purpose is to finish it."

"No, I mean the real purpose of our work, what does it actually do. Maybe even the need of such a thing as a job existing in the first place." The protagonist kept on; he felt better letting his thoughts out. So he continued, "We come here, we do some paperwork, and nobody seems to care; it doesn't seem to have any real meaning. We get paid, I don't know what for. We finish our work and we work again tomorrow, and the same for everyone else. Is this really how it has to be? Is this really the only way? And also, why can't our systems be less complicated? The rules that make them up seem so arbitrary are put in place by an unknown hand, serving only the purpose of making people jump through hoops, even in getting the most menial of work done."

While talking he was once again gazing into empty space, where all these thoughts and words felt like they emanated from, but after finishing he looked up at his face. It was the face of someone who was happily in the dark. It reminded him of the pleasure a dog gets whilst being led on a leash, relishing this semblance of freedom, not really realising how little control it has, not realising that the leash is a sign of servitude, not freedom.

"Well, that's very interesting. I'll check on you after lunch to see if you have finished your part of the paperwork," he said and turned away, leaving the protagonist confounded.

I shouldn't have said that to him, it was foolish, he thought. He decided to be more cautious about his newfound beliefs, as they seemed to enter dead ears. He felt like he was the only sane person on the planet. *Could it be that I am the only one who can see? Is everybody else blind to the true state of things?* He felt sick. A great weariness and nausea attacked him; the loneliness was taking its toll. He wondered if maybe it was better to stay in the dark, happily hopping around the darkness without a care in the world. And while the darkness was filled with contentment and joy, the light burned with passion. It burned so much that a human could barely handle it; it seared his mind and kept it racing, not leaving him a moment's rest. Yet, he decided that the light still was the better place to be. *Maybe this is the price to pay in order to realise, in order to hit the bedrock of reality.*

The lunch bell sounded and his colleagues got out of their chairs in unison, and in unison they walked, perfect copies of each other, each vehemently following the same set of rules. After recuperating for a couple of minutes, the protagonist decided to go get lunch himself.

He remembered that he had a coupon for a free meal at the sandwich shop next door, so he decided to use it. When walking out of the office building, he made sure to keep his gaze focused only on his feet, and on what's in front of him, so as not to see those happy grins on people's faces. He dreaded their smiles, their confused and happy countenance. While walking, he felt as if everyone was looking at him, even though he did not look at the people on the street; he could feel their gaze, as if he was the odd one out, as if he was insane and they all perfectly well off. *I can't take this much longer,* he thought.

Upon entering the sandwich shop, he saw that there was no line which gave him a slight sense of relief. Feeling a bit better, he even forced a smile while talking to the man at the counter.

"I would like to use this coupon for a free meal," the protagonist said.

"Let me see," said the man. He took the coupon and looked at it, "I'm sorry, the coupon is no longer valid."

He gave the coupon back to the protagonist who looked at it in amazement. He checked the expiration date and saw that it wasn't due for another two months. He sternly looked at the man behind the counter and gave him the coupon again.

"It seems to be very valid to me," he said almost hissing through his teeth.

"It's ripped," said the man, refusing to take the coupon.

The protagonist looked at the coupon again. There was the slightest of tears on the side of the coupon; you could barely see it.

"Are you insane? How could you not accept coupons that are so slightly ripped? What am I supposed to do? Keep it in a glass box."

"You could if you wanted to. But I just can't accept it."

"You see, that's where you are wrong; you can accept it, but you just don't want to."

"No. What I want doesn't matter. It's just the protocol."

The protagonist felt like he was on the verge of fainting. He could not believe what he was hearing. *Another idiotic system,* he thought. This time though, he was determined to get his way; he was determined to get to the bottom of this scheme.

"I want to speak to the person who made up this rule and see where it is written," the protagonist proclaimed.

"I can call the manager to speak with you."

The protagonist nodded, fearing that if he tried to speak in reply, he would start screaming. He hesitated at making a scene. He wanted to keep his cool and have a rational conversation about the topic, but his feelings were getting the better of him. He closed his eyes and took two deep breaths in order to calm himself down. When he opened his eyes, he saw a woman coming toward him, smiling amicably.

"Hello, I am the manager. I understand you wish to speak with me," she said politely.

"Well yes," said the protagonist, soothed by her friendly tone. "I hope you can give me an answer to my question."

"Which is?"

"Who made up the system for deciding which coupons are valid and which are not? I just can't understand it. Mine is just a little bit ripped, probably from staying in my pocket for too long. And the man at the counter said that that made it not valid. It seems absurd to me," the protagonist exclaimed very fast, barely catching his breath.

"Well, yes. That is the protocol."

Upon hearing this, the protagonist started getting red in the face; he felt as if the top of his head was about to explode. Seeing this, the manager started speaking again.

"This is not the fault of the man at the counter; he did not make up the rules," she said.

"Well, who did?" yelled the protagonist, "That's what I really want to know. Who makes all these arbitrary, incomprehensible rules?"

"I don't know that either. They seem to have been in place forever as if nobody really put them there. So, asking a question like that would be like asking what came first, the chicken, or the egg."

The protagonist was confounded by this answer. It was the first time today that he heard someone making sense. He looked at the face of the woman again. She still had a semblance of some sort of a happy grin, yet she had a depth in her eyes, and they showed reason. He felt like she had a firm grasp of things, or at least better than most people. Upon realising this, he calmed down and decided that a free sandwich was not worth all the fuss.

"I'll tell you what," he said, "I'm going to go to the cash machine across the street and come back to pay for a sandwich."

"That sounds excellent," she said smiling earnestly, and walked back behind the counter, continuing her work.

Feeling quite a bit better, the protagonist went across the street to the cash machine in order to withdraw funds. He felt so much better that on the way there, he hardly noticed other people or judged their mental states. *Perhaps, I am not as alone as I thought I was,* he thought. He placed the card in the machine, waited a couple of seconds, and immediately realised something was wrong. The machine showed no signs of responding. He started frantically hitting at random buttons, desperate to receive his card back. *Another one,* this thought kept racing through his mind. Some people might not be that bad after all, but these systems seemed irreparable. After a couple of minutes of pressing random buttons, and shaking the machine like a mad man, it displayed a harrowing message: *System failure.* The protagonist couldn't help but force a sardonic smile; the irony was starting to pass the threshold of infuriating to amusing. He noticed that there was also a small piece of text underneath: *Pick up your card at your nearest bank.* He immediately started dreading this occurrence; banks were notorious for their circuitous and incomprehensible systems, and they were seldom easy to reason with. Nevertheless, he needed his card. It made sense to get this tedious task out of the way as soon as possible.

Luckily, a bank was not far away. He had to take a five-minute walk. It seemed like there were not many people in the street. He looked at his clock and noticed that it was way past lunchtime, and that he would be late back to work, again. *Who cares,* he thought, *I know I'm right about working hours being arbitrary. And what are they going to do? Fire me? I don't think so; hardly anyone gets fired.* These thoughts gave him comfort, but he still sped up his step a bit.

He entered the bank and immediately noticed the huge line of smiling, grinning people, happy to oblige to the unspoken rules of in-bank behaviour. *What a load of sheep,* he thought, *carefully being led by an unseen shepherd.* To his great surprise, the guard working at the bank started coming toward him with a wide, sheepish smile.

"Please sir, come right to the front of the line," he said as he pushed his way through the herd of people who seemed not at all bothered by someone cutting in front of them.

Flummoxed by this occurrence, the protagonist could barely come to his senses, and he was already face-to-face with the bank clerk.

"Hello sir," said the clerk, "is this your card?" she asked, dangling his card in front of his nose.

"Yes," said the protagonist and reached out his hand to take the card. However, as soon as he tried to take it, the clerk withdrew it at breakneck speed.

"Well, you will need to fill out some paperwork to get it back," she said smiling, but not with the happy grin displayed by most; her smile was devious and almost demonic.

"Let me guess, that's the protocol."

"Excellent, how did you know?" She said with a rudely ironic tone.

Afterward, she looked him straight in the eyes and clapped her hands. At the sound of the clap, four more office clerks ran out from behind their desks carrying inordinately large sums of paper. They all in unison started throwing the paper at the protagonist's head and yelling instruction about how to fill up the forms. The protagonist felt like drowning; he could hardly breathe from the sheer amount of paper being thrown at his head. He could barely hear anything from the plethora of voices yelling at his ear. He did feel like he could hear something in the background, the sound of people laughing. He immediately thought that he was the source of the laughter, that it was meant for him, and he couldn't help but feel ashamed, even amidst all the commotion. Inside the flurry of paper, he could see an opening. From that opening, like a sign from heaven itself, he could see his card. He clenched his jaw and started marching, determined to get to it. The flurry of paper and voices was not stopping, but he could see himself getting closer. Finally, he touched it; he grabbed the card, but the clerk wasn't letting go. He continued to struggle, the papers still flying everywhere. He pulled and pulled harder and harder, but the other clerks pulled him in the other way. And then, suddenly, he saw a bright light.

Part two

The protagonist woke up with an unrelenting headache. He started rubbing his eyes, and upon feeling out his head, he saw that it was bandaged. Slowly getting back to his senses, he started noticing his surroundings. He was in a small room with concrete walls and bars on one end. It was a prison cell. He tried to collect his thoughts, but the headache wouldn't let him think straight. Trying to remember how he got there, he couldn't really recollect what had happened. He knew he went a little wild at the bank, but it all seemed like a dream, like it wasn't really him. *The guard must have hit me to calm me down,* he thought, *and to think how amicable he was at first. Not only are people confused and unaware, they are also duplicitous.* He remembered the devilish smile of the bank clerk. Upon remembering it, he felt chills. He couldn't discern what it was about her demeanour that made her so eerie; she looked the same as the rest of them. Suddenly he realised, it was her eyes; something in them was different, but he couldn't tell what. His musings were interrupted by a banging on the cell's bars.

"I see you have finally woken up," said the prison guard who did the banging.

"I hope your head doesn't hurt too bad. That guy really got you good," said another guard, leaning on the bars of the cell.

"Am I under arrest? How long will I have to stay here?" asked the protagonist.

"No, you can go as soon as we unlock this door."

"Why did you place me in a jail cell then?"

"That's the protocol. We have to judge if you are sane enough when you wake up. And since you seem so, you're free to go."

The protagonist was shocked that he was presented with an explanation to the workings of a protocol. And, he was even more surprised to find that it actually made sense. Before he knew it, the guards unlocked the cell and helped him out. They gave him some water to drink and checked his bandages. The protagonist was surprised at their good will, but couldn't give it much time because of his headache; it was getting worse.

"Well now, I hope you won't be throwing any more fits in public places," said one of the guards. "What got into you anyway?"

"Yeah, you seem like a normal guy," said the other one.

"I don't know," said the protagonist.

He could barely look at their faces; his vision was starting to get blurry. The guards saw that he was in a bad way and escorted him to a chair. *Is this headache ever going to go away?* thought the protagonist.

"Listen, I think you should go see the doctor again. He already bandaged your head up, but you might need some medication," said the guard worriedly.

"I don't know if I can walk," answered the protagonist wearily.

The two guards took a couple of steps to the side and started whispering to each other. The protagonist couldn't quite work out what they were whispering about; all he could hear was the throbbing of his blood. Through the noise, he could make out some words. He heard them say: "help, why, crazy, protocol..." Words which were unfortunately becoming very familiar to him. The guards had their discussion for quite some time, so much so, that the protagonist dozed off to sleep. It wasn't a deep sleep; it was the type of sleep where you are aware that you are sleeping, a sort of dreamless darkness. Suddenly, one of the guards shook him and the darkness disappeared.

"We will carry you. On this chair. Just don't move too much."

The protagonist nodded, too weary to speak. The guards stood each on one side of the chair and lifted the protagonist with shocking ease. He closed his eyes as the shaking and commotion made him queasy. In the darkness, he could see flashes of light. He could hear the footsteps of the guards. They sounded like they were walking in perfect unison. Again, the darkness was interrupted, this time with a thud. The two guards placed the chair in front of a door.

"From here, you'll have to go it alone," one of them said.

"The doctor's office is just through that door," said the other.

"We can't go in there."

"That's the protocol."

"Thank you for your help," muttered the protagonist.

The two guards looked at each other in bewilderment, as if it was strange for him to thank them, as if it was unnecessary to thank them for something that they must do. Feeling a little better, the protagonist started looking more closely at the two guards standing next to him. He twisted his head from left to right, looking at one then the other. He was shocked to notice that they looked almost identical; their faces seemed to be exactly the same, down to each shape and curve. *Are they twins?* he thought. They looked like two perfectly identical robots, specially engineered for their jobs. As he twisted his head to one side, he saw one guard reaching into his pocket. Out of his pocket, he took out a stack of papers that really seemed too large to fit in it. He very forcibly put the papers in the protagonist's lap, while the other guard placed a pen in his hand.

"You'll have to fill out these forms before we go," they both said, almost simultaneously.

The protagonist was angered by this occurrence, even though he expected something like it. He looked at the faces of the guards again, but saw them changed. Their previous amicable attitude towards him was gone. They were looking at him sternly, fidgeting, and snapping their fingers, anxious for him to finish the task put in front of him. He got frightened by their new appearance and didn't protest but got down to filling out the forms. As soon as he finished, one of the guards snatched the forms and the other the pen at lightning speed. After this, they proceeded to run down the hall away from the protagonist, standing right next to each other, their every motion identical and simultaneous.

Dumbfounded, the protagonist barely gathered up enough strength to get up from the chair. He leaned on the door and turned the handle. Upon turning it, the door violently swung open and he fell face-first onto the floor. The headache was worse than ever. The thumping of blood was beginning to drive him insane and he could not see anymore. Every time he opened his eyes all he could see was a mixture of light and darkness intertwining. He felt like screaming, but the scream was somehow locked inside and couldn't get out. As if it was miles away. He could hear a faint voice comforting him: *There, there. We're going to make you better now.* His vision started coming back and he saw that somebody had placed him on a hospital bed. From the corner of his eye, he could see a needle sticking into his arm. The pain was great; some sort of liquid was pouring through him now. He could feel it coursing through his veins; it was cold. And then suddenly, he realised that the throbbing had stopped; there was no more pain; he opened his eyes. In front of him, the doctor was standing with an empty syringe in his right hand, with the other hand, he was checking the protagonist's pulse.

"He didn't have to hit you that hard," the doctor said.

The protagonist just kept staring at him. Something about the doctor was soothing to him, his presence made him feel safe.

"What sort of medication was that? It worked really fast," asked the protagonist.

"The usual kind, don't worry," answered the doctor, as he sat back in his chair and started swinging in it from side to side and whistling absentmindedly.

The protagonist couldn't take his eyes of the doctor; there was something about him that was puzzling, that was different from everyone else. He certainly wasn't afraid of eye contact. He kept staring right into the eyes of the protagonist as if he was trying to figure him out as well. They sat for some time in the silence like that, enough time for the protagonist to figure out what aspect of the doctor's demeanour was so idiosyncratic: he seemed to be indifferent. Every other person that he met, especially on that day had some sort of underlying agenda about them, some sort of stance and attitude, even himself. But he was different because of his staunch disapproval of every type of system; the doctor was different because he looked like he didn't care whether a system existed or not.

"Am I free to go now?" asked the protagonist timidly, still in awe of the presence of the doctor.

"Certainly," said the doctor. "But I was hoping I could talk to you."

"About what?"

"Well, you have been making quite a name for yourself, stories of your deeds have been passing through the channels."

"What channels?" baffled, the protagonist blurted out.

"The usual kind," said the doctor with a smile, proceeding to look at the protagonist as if studying him. "Your physical health is not a great mystery and will remain fine; the medicine you got is to thank for that, and the guard is to thank for you needing any medicine in the first place. However, I would like to have a chat about your other health, perhaps the even more important type of health," this he said while touching his forehead with his forefinger.

"If you think I am insane you are mistaken," said the protagonist, insulted by the insinuation. "It is everybody else you should be examining."

"Oh, heavens no! I didn't even think of the former, but I would like you to expound the latter."

The protagonist hesitated. Each time he tried to communicate his feelings to somebody he wound up regretting it. People didn't seem to be ready for the truth which he realised. But something about the doctor gave him hope that he might have found an adequate listener, and more importantly, someone who would actively contribute to the conversation with his own ideas. He decided to proceed slowly. To try and figure out if his hunch was correct along the way.

"The systems we have in place are nonsense," he said, staring at the ground, not knowing what to expect.

"Some of them, certainly."

At this the protagonist raised his head, his eyes gleaming with hope. He opened his mouth but words failed to come out.

"When did this revelation come to you?" asked the doctor.

"Today," the protagonist said, retaining his ability to speak. "You wouldn't believe the day I have been having."

"Well, as I said, I know some of it. And by the injury you sustained, I can understand your frustration. But do you wonder, what is the root of your frustration? What are you really angry about? Is it the system?"

"I don't follow," the protagonist was genuinely confused. "Of course it's the system. We as a society have made these huge mistakes in building the scheme of things. Nothing seems to make any sense; everything is arbitrary, and even without any explanation, people seem happy to follow along. It drives me crazy."

"True. Sometimes, these things don't make sense; sometimes people do not know why they do something the way they do, and they rarely question it."

"Yes exactly," the protagonist exclaimed excitedly.

"But," the doctor stopped him from continuing to speak. "That still isn't the true reason for your anger."

"Then what is?" the protagonist was starting to get annoyed by all the mysterious leads and insinuations, "Tell me straight."

"You are angry with yourself."

This sentence hit like a bullet. With no warning, it made an eternal wound.

"What do you mean by that?" the protagonist asked, this time pleadingly.

"You are angry because you didn't figure this out earlier. Because only yesterday, you were a member of the happy bunch, mindlessly following the rules," the doctor saw that the protagonist had trouble stomaching his words. So, he made a pause, stood up, walked to the window, and staring out of it, continued, "We humans are innately selfish little creatures. Our ego does everything it can in order to protect us from our own mistakes and imperfections. Thus, when we realise a tragic flaw in ourselves, our ego does everything in its power to project that flaw onto something else. Sometimes, that something else is a person, sometimes many people, and sometimes society at large." These last words he said turning his head to the protagonist and walking to the hospital bed; he sat by his side.

Now, the protagonist was the one looking into empty space. He tried to get his thoughts in order. *Is he right? Am I the problem?* he thought. He knew that the doctor could be right; everything he said made a lot of sense, and he seemed like a man who was in the know. He turned to the doctor looking pleadingly, hoping that he will give him some relief.

"This isn't something to get too stressed about," said the doctor, noticing his look. "It's just part of your programming. You could say it is part of the protocol," he said with a devilish smile.

"Even if that is true," said the protagonist coming back to his senses, "That doesn't mean that I'm not right."

"Of course not, you most certainly are."

"So, you can see it too?"

The doctor nodded. He then stood up again and went back to his chair and started swinging in it once again.

"Do you want me to tell you a personal story?" he asked.

"Yes."

"It's rather long."

"I don't mind."

"Okay then," he took a deep breath, then continued, "at one point in time, I felt exactly the same way you do now. I was disillusioned by society, thought of it as stupid and couldn't help but express my feelings to anyone and everyone. Unfortunately, I too, met deaf ears, and nobody seemed to care. I felt so alone. I wanted to change everything, especially the way people thought. Not because I wanted to make something better but because I couldn't stand being so alone. Being completely alone is one thing, but being alone while in the company of many is an even more harrowing experience. When you are alone amongst many, you cannot help but feel hope that your state of loneliness will cease and somebody else will come to their senses alongside you. But it is very foolish to think so. Eventually, I got disillusioned even with my hopes. I came to the understanding that I will never be able to make anyone see. In my hubris, I ascribed my failure as to everyone else's fault. I thought that people were to blame for being too blind. And for not being able to see. Not once did it cross my mind how hard it is to come to the realisations that I had come to. What an arduous task it was for me as well. Indignantly, I looked at everyone as fools, and the more indignant, the sadder I grew. Eventually, I decided that people and society didn't deserve my wisdom, which they didn't want in the first place. I decided to go from them, far away, to live as a hermit. An ascetic life where I shall make the rules and not be subject to the stupid rules followed by many. And so, I lived for quite some time, alone in the wilderness, providing for myself and not caring for anything but myself. At first, it was amazing; I felt so free, so peaceful, nobody there to tell me what I ought to do. But then I had too much time to think, and in thinking I discovered the secret games of my own ego. I discovered that I was fooling myself all along. I was not, and am not in fact, special. The revelations that I had come by were accessible to all, and I was not the first to have them. More importantly, I realised that I had no better idea of how to run things. I couldn't think of any systems of my own to replace the existing ones, making all my anger and disgust null and void. I was as lost as everyone else. So, I decided to return and since then, the thoughts that you are now having have not been disturbing me anymore. Of course, now and then I get a pang of pain at seeing something done in a nonsensical way, but I accept it. I accept the world as it is, and I am not on a crusade to change it. Maybe it can be changed; maybe I'm just too weak to do it. Perhaps. But not trying to change it has made me much more content and less lonely.

And in the grand scheme of things, the real scheme of things, isn't that all that matters? That we are free of worry and in good company. I know this sounds too prosaic and a tad bit like a platitude, but I have had a lot of time to think about it, and to me, it seems to be the truth."

Upon finishing his monologue, the doctor sat up and went to the window again. The protagonist didn't quite know how he should answer; he didn't really know what to think of what he had just heard. Sure, it made sense, but it did little to quench any of his own anger or disillusionment. Perhaps it was one of those things that you need to feel for yourself. Perhaps, in time, he would come to the same conclusions. But for now, a fire was still burning in him, and no amount of words or advice could do anything to put it out.

"Well, what do you think?" asked the doctor, interrupting the protagonist's thoughts, "Is my advice any valid?"

"It makes sense," said the protagonist. "But it doesn't really answer all my questions."

"As I suspected. The ineffable cannot be explained, no matter how many words you use. You have learned that today for sure."

They stayed in the room for some time like that in silence. Both of them wished to keep on talking, but the words seemed to be swallowed by the silence.

"You are free to go if you wish." The doctor was the first one to break the silence.

"Let me guess. I'm going to have to fill out some forms."

"No. Who has time for such silly things. Forms and paperwork are just arbitrary anyway, right?" the doctor turned to the protagonist and gave a warm smile.

"Thank you," said the protagonist and left the office.

He went outside to the street with his mind filled with confusing thoughts once again. *What should I do with all this knowledge I have acquired today,* mused the protagonist. He particularly liked the idea of being a hermit. It didn't occur to him until the doctor mentioned his own travails as one, but somehow, the protagonist thought that he could do it better. He felt that if done right, an ascetic life with no system to it at all could be the answer. *It seems possible,* he thought. He wondered about the question of loneliness, so glaringly brought up by the doctor and figured that there was no need to live all alone, far from society. Maybe some people would like to join him. *There must be a lot of people fed up with everything,* and the doctor's similar views seemed to prove it. *But not too many,* he thought, a*n optimal number needs to be found.* Everything larger than this number would start inadvertently needing systems, which seemed to feed on large gatherings of people and take them over. He started feeling very merry at these thoughts, living out in the woods with his own band of like-minded followers. They would have a new start, a new beginning, and they would be the masters of their own destiny. No rules, no troubles, just people living as they were destined to before the interruption of systems and norms.

He kept on wandering down the streets, looking very attentively at people. All of them seemed to have the sheepish, happy grin that he had grown so accustomed to. Yet, this didn't make him lose his spirit. He knew that he would eventually find the compatriots he was looking for and that they would be happy to join him in his plans. A new sort of enthusiasm filled his mind. He could barely contain himself from smiling. He noticed that people in the street started giving him odd looks, but he did not care. The looks rolled over him as he was dead set on his new path. Soon, he would no longer be alone.

"You are not alone."

He heard the voice barely, and could not figure out where it was coming from. He frantically started turning from side to side and saw a shadowy figure standing in a dark corner of a deserted alley. The figure beckoned him.

"Who are you?" the protagonist asked, timidly coming closer to the figure.

"A like-minded individual," the figure replied.

The protagonist was lost for words. *Is this really happening? Are my hopes coming true so soon?* he thought. Free from all fear and certain that he had found what he was looking for, he came very close to the dark figure.

"Like-minded how?" asked the protagonist.

"You know how."

"Yes, I do," the protagonist started smiling. "When did you come to the realisation?"

"A long time ago, we are looking for new members."

"We?"

"Yes, there is more of us than you think. And soon we will act."

The protagonist could barely contain his joy. He started laughing heartily and loudly. He looked at the figure and saw that he was smiling as well. *Finally, somebody who completely makes sense,* he thought. He felt safe and finally in good company, in company that understood him.

"Would you like to join?" the man finally asked.

"Yes."

"Come with me, we are having a meeting right now."

The protagonist followed the mysterious man down the dark alley. At the end of the alley, there was a door they went through. As soon as they went through the door, there was a winding staircase. The protagonist looked down and couldn't see where it ended. He also noticed that there were no lights. He looked around and saw that the man had already started going down, not looking back. He ran after him in the dark, careful not to stumble. Upon catching him, he grabbed him by the shoulder and turned him around. The man just put his finger to the protagonist's lips, showing him that he should hush up. Carefully, the protagonist kept following him down the stairs, which were now completely in the dark. He minded his step so as not to fall down and noticed that the man was walking incredibly fast, considering it was pitch dark by now. Finally, he started seeing a dim light; it was coming from down under. And soon, they reached the end of the long winding staircase. He could now hear voices which seemed to be coming from the end of the hall in which they were now standing. He closed his eyes, getting used to the well-lit hall after some time in the dark. When he opened them, he saw the man standing next to a door at the end of the hall, beckoning him. He could still hear the voices.

As soon as he entered the room, the voices stopped. He saw a semicircle of people sitting on chairs, and they were all looking straight at him. One of them stood up.

"We have been waiting for you," they said.

"Who are you?" asked the protagonist, losing a bit of his former enthusiasm.

"We are like-minded people."

"I heard that already. But what do you do?"

"We will overturn the system."

At saying this, the crowd of people started cheering. The protagonist felt like cheering as well, but he contained himself. He wanted to figure out more about what this group of people was about.

"And how do you plan to do that?" he asked.

"We will tear it down with no mercy," said a person who was obviously the leader, followed by another cheer from the crowd. "We will break down these archaic, nonsensical principles, and build new, sane ones in their stead. No more shall people have to follow arbitrary rules; no more shall we kowtow to excessively unexplainable demands. We will suffer no longer and will usher in a utopia, a society without a system where anyone is free to follow their heart and their own wits. Yes, we shall do this soon, and it shall be glorious!"

Another cheer followed. This time, the protagonist joined the cheering. He had heard all he needed to. He knew that these were people who were to be trusted, who understood the true state of things. He felt a sudden release, the pent-up loneliness was gone.

"How can I help?" he asked smiling wildly.

"First, you will have to join and say an oath of allegiance, and then, we will decide which task to give you. However, judging by your deeds today, the task will not be a small one. You will have a great part to play in what is to come."

The protagonist felt elated. *Finally, somebody can see my worth,* he thought.

"When do we start?" he asked, with an inerasable smile forming on his face.

"Soon, but first, you will have to fill out these forms."

The room started spinning. The smile disappeared from the protagonist's face. He tried to speak, but he started choking, he could hear his heart beating in his head again. Frantically, he started looking at the faces of the people in the room more closely. He nearly vomited once he noticed it, once he noticed the happy grins on each of their faces. Smiling like there is no care in the world. It was painfully clear that these were not the like-minded people that he was looking for all along. He looked at the leader standing in front of him, holding out a stack of forms, and smiling devilishly. He wanted to scream, but the sound didn't come out. He wanted to run, but his legs wouldn't move. The leader was moving closer, pen and paper in hand. Finally, he came to his senses, knocked the paper out of the leader's hands and started running out of the room. He ran as fast as he could down the hallway and up the dark staircase. It seemed to him like he made it to the top of the staircase with incredible speed, considering it seemed like it took a lifetime to get down.

Everything was moving faster. Out of breath, he came out into the alley and back into the street. Running mindlessly and trying to outrun his thoughts. *Am I really all alone?* this thought kept racing through his head as tears formed in his eyes. He felt lost, lost and alone. He noticed that people on the street started looking at him rather worriedly; some of them started coming near him, but he shoved them away and kept running. While running, he looked at everything around him. Everywhere he could see lines, lines of people with their happy grins, filling out paperwork. Not a care in the world. He kept running. As he looked more attentively, he could see the bodies of people morphing as if they were becoming sheep and monkeys. He screamed, this time out loud. More people started looking at him worriedly. But he kept running. While running, he got tangled up in something like a spider web. He jerked and shook, but he couldn't get out. Pulling on the strings, he saw that they were attached to other people. Attached to their backs, legs, arms, and faces. He screamed once more. *They are all puppets!* With this thought, he shook harder and broke free from the strings. He kept running. Suddenly, he heard a screech, and then he saw dark.

Part three

The protagonist woke up in a dimly lit grey room. He was lying on the floor. He slowly stood up expecting another massive headache but it never came. *Where am I?* he wondered as he noticed that there were no people around him. Recovering his wits, he started looking for a way out of the room. The dim lighting was hurting his eyes. He was shocked to find that the room had no door; neither did it have any windows, even stranger; he couldn't find the source of the dim light. It was as if it was a part of the air in the room. He spent quite some time in that room. All alone, desperately trying to find a way out. Even worse, he couldn't figure out what had happened and wished for anybody to be there so that he wouldn't be quite so alone.

"You're finally awake."

The protagonist jumped in fear when he heard the voice coming from behind him. And upon turning, he saw a mysterious figure clad in white. He looked carefully at it, but the white garments shone in great contrast to the dim lighting, so he could not discern much. All that he could see was that the figure was wearing a hood which was covering its face.

"Who are you?" asked the protagonist.

"That is difficult to answer," answered the mysterious figure.

"Can you at least tell me where I am?"

"Another question with a very complicated answer."

The figure did not seem very interested in answering the protagonist's questions. In fact, it didn't seem very interested in anything at all. After getting used to the sharp contrast in brightness between the figure and the rest of the room, the protagonist noticed that the figure had a very lackadaisical stance as if this were a part of some kind of everyday, prosaic task. He realised that he would not get a straight answer to his questions, and that he would have to be the one to instigate any sort of conversation.

"Can I get out of here?" the protagonist asked.

"Yes."

"How? I don't see a door."

"You will not need a door."

"Then how will I get out?"

"You will know when the time comes."

"Are you some sort of prison guard? Is this a jail cell? Did I break some rule again and am now declared a menace to society?"

"No."

The protagonist was getting angry. He couldn't seem to get any type of straightforward answer. He started walking around the room once again, hoping to find an exit by himself.

"You will not find an exit," said the figure.

"What am I supposed to do when you don't answer any of my questions?"

"Ask the right questions."

The protagonist stood and tried to think of a solution. He couldn't figure out what was at hand when suddenly the answer seemed obvious.

"Do you want me to accept the system before you let me out?" he asked very confidently.

"No."

After this, the protagonist got really mad. He started punching the walls and screaming, letting all the rage that was building up from the entirety of the day seep out. *Damn these people! Damn them all! I will not accept anything which seems absurd to me! They can't make me*! thus his thoughts raged in his head.

"Think about what you last remember before you got here," the figure suddenly said.

"I was with that gathering of people, who I thought would be my allies, but turned out to be the same as the rest," said the protagonist sadly.

"Feelings are not what is important here, think about facts."

"Facts?"

"Raw facts and sensations."

The protagonist started thinking. He realised that a lot of his memories were actually blurred by his emotions and had trouble discerning what the actual facts were.

"I was running," he said.

"And?"

"I was mad."

"That is a feeling. Facts."

"I was running across the street," said the protagonist, annoyed by the correction, when suddenly he froze and his mouth got dry. "I heard something high pitched, and then I was here."

"Yes."

"Was I in an accident? Am I badly hurt? Am I in a coma and dreaming?" the protagonist blurted out in a frenzy.

"No."

The protagonist took some time to think. He already knew the answer but dreaded hearing the confirmation. He felt that if he never asked it would never actually be true.

"Am I dead?" Finally, he summoned up the courage to ask.

"Yes."

The room started spinning. The protagonist sat, leaning on the wall, and put his head to his knees. He felt like crying but didn't seem to be able to. All he could do was look straight ahead; his mind empty. He never quite imagined what it would be like to be dead or to die, to not be anymore. It seemed to him preposterous to imagine a world where he does not exist, as it does to all humans. He wondered if this was another trick that the human ego plays on people. And after a while, he seemed to ponder nothing at all; his mind was very clear. He sat there for a while, and then a thought sprang to his head.

"What is next?" he asked, realising this was not the end because he was here even though he was dead.

"You will find out in time."

"Still no straight answers?" the protagonist went back to being annoyed.

"You don't ask straight question. You ask complex and abstract questions which would take an age to truly answer."

"How do you mean?"

"There you go again."

The protagonist gave up on further questioning and finally decided to stand up. He stood very close to the hooded figure when a sudden realisation popped into his mind.

"Are you God?" he asked, regretting his former indignant attitude.

"No."

"Then what are you? An angel? Or the devil?"

"Neither. It is only humans who have the need to have such clear-cut definitions for everything. There are no demons or angels. I am just a gatekeeper."

"Well, is there a God?"

"If you have to put a name to it, then yes. Yes, there is."

"I always thought all of that was just a myth, made up so that people can sleep sounder at night."

"It is."

"You just said that God is real."

"That which you call so is real, but all the stories which you tell are still only stories."

Perplexed with all this new information, the protagonist felt the need to sit down again. He looked around the room again for a comfortable place to sit, but there was no such place. There was nothing there.

"I wish heaven had more comfortable furniture," he said.

"This isn't what you would call heaven."

"Then what is it?" the protagonist was encouraged in his rage by the fact that the figure was not as divine as he thought, *Where am I? And when can I finally get out?*

"Right now."

"Really?"

"Yes."

"Then what was the point of all of this?"

"It is my job."

"To do what?"

"To make sure that you are not too despondent and useless. Sometimes it takes a while for people to stomach the fact that their earthly existence is over. You got over it pretty quick. You must be very prone to chasing ideals. You must be very excited to see if somebody will explain the order of things to you."

"Will they?"

"Soon."

"And why did I have to wait such a long time for you to arrive?"

"I had business with other people. You are not the only one."

"Couldn't you have made a better schedule so that I didn't have to wait?"

"I don't make the schedule."

"Then who does?"

"Nobody. It just is."

The protagonist shuddered slightly at this final answer. He started fearing that his questions would go unanswered.

"So, why am I still here then?" he asked.

"I have to double check if you are ready."

"Why?"

"It's the protocol."

And before the protagonist had a chance to react in disgust and rage, he was suddenly in another room. This time, the room was all white and brightly lit. He could barely see without squinting, but he soon got used to it. He proceeded to look around this room as well, but it was as empty as the last one. *When will somebody explain what is happening? What am I to do?* he thought in his misery. He felt that the answers he was looking for were close at hand, but he was impatient to get a hold of them.

"Soon you will find out what you are to do."

The voice resonated, echoing from the walls of the room. The protagonist looked behind, expecting to find another figure standing behind him, but there wasn't one. He looked around the room in fear, but there was no one.

"Who said that?" he felt funny talking into thin air.

"That is very difficult to answer."

"I guess you can't tell me where I am either," said the protagonist, annoyed with all the riddles.

"You learn fast."

"And I guess that I am the one who will have to ask all the questions, if I am to get an answer."

To this he heard only silence in reply. It seemed that this time, he had an even less talkative companion. He just wished that he could put a face to the sounds. Nevertheless, he took some time in order to carefully plan out his course of questioning. He was determined to stay there as little as possible and get as many answers as possible.

"Are you God?" he finally asked.

"Some would say so."

"And what do you call yourself?"

"Nothing."

This answer confused the protagonist. Nevertheless, he felt a great sense of awe. He was in the presence of God, the God. He quickly realised that this was his chance to get the answers he wished for, and get them quickly.

"What is the purpose of people? If we live after we die, what is the purpose of our life?" he asked.

"To live."

"And what is the purpose of that?"

"To be."

"I don't quite understand. Is this all that I am going to get? Half answers and riddles?"

"You wish for too much."

"Well, you know all the answers. Why can't you just tell me all I wish to know?"

"That's not true."

"What do you mean?" the protagonist was dumbfounded.

"That is just something that is ascribed to the mythologised figure of your imagination. The questions you pose do not have answers as straightforward as you like."

The protagonist took some time again in order to regroup. For some reason, he felt that he had no more time left. He felt in a hurry, his thoughts rushing. So, he decided to seek the answer to his most pressing question.

"Am I right? You know about what," he said with an air of confidence.

"Yes."

"Finally! So, the systems of society are arbitrary?"

"Yes."

The protagonist felt as if a huge weight that he had been carrying around the entire day had fallen from his shoulders. Finally, he received the acceptance that he wished for. He felt like a fool no more. Somebody gave him recognition, and not just anybody. But something started troubling him, a thought, gnawing at his mind.

"But wait," he said, "if you know this, why don't you change it?"

"Your curiosity truly knows no bounds. I give you the answer you have been so arduously searching for, and immediately, you think of another."

"That doesn't answer my question."

"No, it doesn't. I see that you need more work. Your kind ascribes great powers to their deities, and it has been so since the days of your inception. They have many names, they are many, or they are one. But they are always the ones who control all. However, that is not so. You see, those systems that you so loathe have been here since the very beginning, ever-present. They were not created; they were there even before, almost as if they were infinite. They are arbitrary, and they are sometimes a nuisance, but they are essential nonetheless. If you were to take them away, the whole universe would crumble. The same goes for your society. Some of you get disillusioned by this. You start loathing it, but you are merely loathing the stuff that is the matter of your own existence. Every cell in your body, every particle in the universe, follows a system; that is the micro, and this continues endlessly into the macro. You think that these rules are arbitrary, and you are right. But they are rules nonetheless. They are laws that cannot be undone. Nothing can run without this system of things; everything needs to be in place, no matter how boring that may seem. And this is all because these systems are what came first. They are the primordial beings, and everything else came after. So, they are in control, and everything else must merely keep it flowing, or chaos ensues."

"Can't you change this?" asked the protagonist with tears forming in his eyes.

"As was already said, it was not made, nor is it known what made it. It is as if this scheme of things emanated from within its own itself. So, it cannot be changed. The best anybody can do is follow along."

"So that's it?"

"What ought there be?"

"The entire universe is just a giant bureaucracy? I need something more. This just isn't enough," said the protagonist, who was wailing by now.

"Well, it is all there is, all the same."

The protagonist stretched out on the floor and kept on crying. He dreaded that he ever tried finding any type of answer. He cursed his disillusionment. He cried for the loneliness that was larger than ever before. Now, he was truly alone, not just among men, but among gods, among the entire universe. He wished he would die, only to realise that he already did.

"I don't like this heaven," he muttered wearily.

"You're not supposed to. You are supposed to complete your task."

"A task? In heaven?"

"Heaven is but a concept. Of course there is a task. Everything has a task in the system."

"What is your task?"

"To make sure you complete yours."

"Charming. And I guess talking to you is just part of the protocol?"

"Yes."

"And what is my task?"

Suddenly he found himself in a new room altogether. This one was larger than the others, with proper furniture. *I guess I'm supposed to live here,* the protagonist thought. He went around the room exploring it, before he found a peculiar apparatus in the corner. It had two wooden handles. He picked them up and saw that they had strings connected to them, very long and thin strings. Following the strings, he saw them run out of a hole in the corner, barely large enough to look through, so he knelt and looked down. Way down under he could see figures, no larger than ants-walking forwards and backwards. Upon further examination, he saw that these were people. He saw them walking and each one of them had a path drawn in front of them that they were oblivious to, but he could now see it. He also saw that each one of them had strings connected to them, connected to their arms, legs, back, and face. Surely enough, he saw the man to which the strings he was controlling were connected. He saw him stray from his path, wandering left and right instead of forward and backward. He saw him, and he pulled.

The End.

Made in the USA
Monee, IL
07 July 2026

56552417R00030